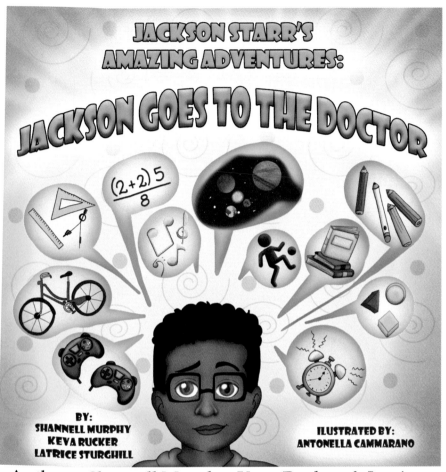

Authors: Shannell Murphy, Keva Rucker, & Latrice Sturghill

Illustrations by: Antonella Cammarano

Edited by: Dr. Kala Rucker Jordan

Acknowledgement/ Dedication

Acknowledgement

We would like to humbly acknowledge our children and co-authors- Kasey, Chelcey, Karter, and Princeton. They have taught us unconditional love. We would like to extend our gratitude to Dr. Kala Rucker Jordan, our editor, and Antonella Cammarano, our illustrator. We are most humbly thankful for the opportunity to have our combined ideas manifest into something real. We would like to honor one another for our vision, time, dedication, and commitment to this project.

Dedication

To all the kids who are struggling with ADHD this is for you! Be cool, have fun, and no worries. It's a very common diagnosis and it doesn't have to keep you from being you, nor does it have to keep you from accomplishing all of the things that you want to accomplish in your lifetime. Work hard, stay encouraged, you're not alone, and help is available to you. Don't be ashamed, don't be embarrassed, let your super powers shine!

Hello, my name is Jackson Starr. I am 9 years old and I'm in the 3rd grade at Sallie Mae Elementary School. I live with my mom, Daisy, my dad, Jacob, and my older sister, Mackenzie. I will tell you about my family later. First, I want to tell you a little bit about myself. I like to dance, play all kinds of sports, and I love school. I love to learn, but sometimes learning seems harder for me than it does for some of the other kids in my class. I also love spending time with my friends and family, especially my cousins, Morgan and Marcell. We are more like sisters and brothers than cousins.

I try so hard to be helpful, but sometimes I feel like being helpful is just me being in the way. I am kind, I tell the truth, I'm fair, I'm honest, and I usually say what's on my mind. I have a big heart, I love everyone, and everyone seems to love me too. I play soccer, basketball, and baseball. I'm not the best athlete, but I have realized that it's not about being the best, but it's about doing your best and having fun while you do it.

At school, I have some girls who think I'm nice and cute, but they just make me blush and feel somewhat shy. So, with all of these great things going on in my life you could say life is good and "I'm the little man around here!!" Unfortunately, there is this one thing, my mom and my teachers say that I'm so full of energy that I have a hard time concentrating. Concentrate is a big word which means to focus. But what do they expect from a growing, 9-year-old boy? It is so hard to focus when there are so many things going on all at once.

I just think boys are made with a lot of energy. My friends, whom I like to call my side kicks, Kody and Miles even have a lot of energy! They are hyper, they tell jokes, they dance, and have fun too! Even my cousins, Marcell, Liam, Dylan, and Julius have a lot of energy. So why am I the only one who is not able to concentrate and have a lot of energy?

My mom and my teachers, Ms. Miller and Ms. Sturgess, say my energy is a little different from the energy that some of the other kids have. Ms. Miller said that I have a hard time sitting still, but who wants to sit still for 10 minutes straight anyway? I like to stand up, stretch, and move around. She said that I have a hard time concentrating which makes it harder for me to learn things in class.

How can I not be distracted with birds chirping outside, kids moving around and laughing, people walking back and forth down the hallway, school announcements coming over the intercom, the sun shining so brightly outside, and the teacher in the front of the class talking about who knows what?! I guess they are right! I'm so easily distracted and I do have a hard time focusing. But what does all of this mean?

I usually go see Dr. Wright when I'm sick with a cold. He's nice and all, but who really likes going to the doctor? Every time I have to go to the doctor, I have anxiety which means I get really nervous and sometimes I start sweating and shaking. I always envision myself having to get a shot! I hate shots!!! And who is the new doctor that he will refer me to? I don't want to see a new doctor; I really like Dr. Wright. Oh brother, it's not easy being 9!

I was a little embarrassed about the idea of something being wrong with me. What would my friends think? What would they say about me? I realized that I have great friends and I needed to talk to them before I exploded, literally! So, I talked to my best friends, Kody and Miles. Miles said "It's okay bro, Dr. Wright will take good care of you. He's cool and he always gives me some kind of treat before I leave every doctor visit." Kody said, "Don't worry, your mom loves you and she would not do anything that would hurt you. So, if she feels that you need to go to the doctor, just trust that it is for your own good." My friends always have a way of cheering me up!

They were right, it will not hurt for me to go and talk to Dr. Wright and get a referral to see another doctor. It will only help me to get better so that I can concentrate, sit still, and focus. But what will he do to me? Will he have a fancy x-ray machine that will look inside of my brain? Will there be some elaborate equipment that he will have to look at all of my energy and can't focus cells? How will he be able to tell what is going on with me? There are so many questions swirling around in my head!

I went home and wanted to talk to my older sister, Mckenzie. Despite our constant arguments and fights, we still love each other. She's a great person for me to talk to because she always seems to give me good advice. Like that one time when I talked to her about a girl that I liked in my class and that time I thought mom and dad were going to be mad at me but Mckenzie told me exactly what to do in order to stay on my parents' good side. She says that I annoy her, but what 9-year old little brother doesn't annoy his teenage sister? She's a teenager, so in my eyes she has been through some things in her life; she has even made her way to high school. She's also a "professional" at handling mom and dad, since she's older.

I went to Mckenzie's room and she was on her phone talking to her friends, Brooklyne and Olivia. Her friends think I'm cute, so I annoy them too. "I will wait until you're done." I said. McKenzie saw that I was not going to leave until she got off the phone, so she finally got off the phone. "What's up Jackson?" she said. "Mom, Ms. Miller, and Ms. Sturgess said that I need to go see Dr. Wright to get a referral and I'm really scared. They said I have too much energy, I can't sit still, I'm easily distracted, and I can't concentrate. What's wrong with me? I'm going to be the laughing stock at school and everyone is going to make fun of me if they think something is wrong with me. I'm doomed, my life is over at the tender age of 9!"

"Calm down Jackson. It's really not that serious. You are who you are and everyone loves you just the way you are. Dr. Wright and the new doctor will probably just talk to you and prescribe you some medicine that will help you focus. You probably just have Attention Deficit Hyperactivity Disorder or ADHD for short. There are plenty of people at my school who have a similar condition, it's nothing to be ashamed of or embarrassed about. Even some adults have ADHD. It is not a huge problem because they make medicine for that. And the medicine will just help you focus better so you can learn all of the things that you need to learn. I would venture to say everyone has ADHD sometimes."

As I listened to McKenzie, I did start to feel better, my heartbeat had slowed down and I started to feel calmer. She went on to say "Besides mom and dad love you and they would not do anything that they thought would hurt you or not be good for you. So, trust their decision on this. Ms. Miller and Ms. Sturgess adore you; they just want to see you do well in school and Dr. Wright is the coolest doctor ever. I'm sure whoever he refers you to will be just as great as he is. You are in good hands, no worries Jackson!!" Mckenzie was right, I really was in good hands. I have a lot of people who love me and I know they only want the best for me. I'm just going to go and talk to Dr. Wright so we can get down to the bottom of what is causing me to be so distracted and energetic.

It was the day to go see Dr. Wright, and even though I had my pep talks, I was honestly still a little nervous. I kept telling myself, "Everything is going to be just fine. I'm in good hands. This is for my own good." Wow, this positive self-talk is really helping me feel better and calm down. My mom, dad, and I walked in to see Dr. Wright. While we waited for the doctor to come in, my parents comforted me and reassured me that everything was going to be great. The doctor came in and he listened to me share my feelings. He actually listened to my concerns and answered all of my questions. He told me that it sounds like I have exactly what Mckenzie said, that really long phrase that's ADHD for short. Wow, Mckenzie is smarter than I give her credit for; she was right!

Dr. Wright said that he was going to refer me to one of his really good friends, whose office is a few blocks down the street. He said that his friend is a Pediatric Psychiatrist. A Pediatric Psychiatrist is a doctor who can prescribe medicine to kids who struggle with emotional and mental disorders. Dr. Wright said that ADHD is a brain condition that is characterized by inattention, hyperactivity, and impulsivity. "Dr. Wright, what does inattention, hyperactivity, and impulsivity mean? I don't understand those terms."

Dr. Wright explained that inattention is basically when a person has difficulty staying focused. They can be disorganized in their thoughts, but it doesn't mean that they are defiant, that they don't understand nor comprehend, nor that they can't learn. Due to them not being able to focus, it makes learning a little more difficult for them, but not impossible. It doesn't mean that they are dumb, they just have to work harder to focus so they are able to learn. "Did that make sense to you?" asked Dr. Wright. "Yes, I understand that, now what about the other two words?"

"Hyperactivity is when a person moves around a lot and has a difficult time staying or sitting still. It is when a person has a lot of activity going on; they are restless, often fidgeting, and talking. Alright Jackson, the last one is impulsivity" said Dr. Wright. "It is a big word for doing things without thinking about it before hand. It's when a person makes decisions without thinking about the potential consequences." Dr. Wright said this is a very common condition for kids and many adults struggle with it too. So, you see it's not that bad, it's definitely not life threatening, I'm going to live and I'm going to be just fine.

Dr. Wright said that I may have to take medicine that will help
me with all of these things, and I will also need to change my
diet, or the things that I eat. He said that my diet is very
important as well. He said that I will need to reduce the
amount of sugar and sweets that I eat as well as the amount of
caffeine that I drink. Oh brother, but I love sugar!! My mom
said that I can have it in moderation, which means I don't
have to completely give it up. I just have to reduce how much
and how often I eat things that have a lot of sugar. Also, I
need to stay away from foods and drinks with red dye. So, no
more red fruit punch for me.

Dr. Wright gave us a referral and sent us on our way. I have to admit, I feel like a huge weight has been lifted off my shoulders, knowing that my condition is manageable with some minor changes. And I don't feel embarrassed about it anymore because there is comfort in knowing that many people struggle with the same issues. I'm happy to know that with the right treatment, my symptoms will decrease, and I will be able to focus, sit still, and finally be able to learn just like the rest of the kids in my class. I was thinking that I was dumb and not capable of learning, but now I know why. Knowing is half the battle, so now I can get proper treatment. I'm not dumb after all, thank goodness! (Insert happy dance).

It was the day to go to see Dr. Wright's friend, Dr. Murphy. She was a female doctor. I knew I would like her because when I met her, she immediately gave me a fist pump and she even blew it out! "How cool is that!" She immediately grabbed my attention because she was trying to relate to me and I liked that. This was going to be the beginning of a beautiful relationship. I needed her to help me get better so I would have to follow "the doctor's orders." She basically confirmed everything that McKenzie and Dr. Wright had said about me. She explained ADHD, just as Dr. Wright explained it. And she didn't have to use any fancy equipment to examine my brain. She just listened to me as I explained the things that I have been going through. She said all of my symptoms are exactly that of ADHD.

She said that the thing about taking medicine for mental or brain conditions is that sometimes you have to take or even try different medications until you find one that works best for you. "Everyone's body is different and medications don't work the same for everyone," she said. She asked me to be patient with her and work with her during this process. She said this is definitely going to be a team effort with her, my parents, my teachers, and me. We will all need to work together to ensure that I get better. She said that it's important for everyone on the team to do their part in order for the team to be successful. With that being said, she prescribed me a medication to try.

She said that I would have to give it a few weeks before I
started to see any results and that I may have some side
effects. But she said that I needed to keep a list of how I'm
feeling while taking the medication. So, she gave me a
journal! My very first journal. She said that I could choose to
write in it every day or every other day, just a few sentences of
how I'm feeling and if I've noticed any changes going on in
my body. But there is one thing about the medication, it's not
the cute little gummies that I'm used to taking, it's an actual
pill. I've never taken a pill before. Dr. Murphy said that I'm
going to have to get creative with ways to take this cute little
pill. So here we go!

My name is Jackson Starr and I have ADHD. I have ADHD but it does not define me! It's not who I am. I'm not incapable of learning, I am not a weirdo, I am not contagious, I don't have a yucky disease, I am not unlovable, I am not unlikeable. I just have to take a pill to help me focus and sit still at school so that I can learn. It's not my fault or anything that I have done wrong, it's nothing to be ashamed of nor embarrassed about. I'm uniquely Jackson and I love who I am!! I'm on this new adventure, living life and managing my ADHD. Stay tuned for all of my new life's adventures living with ADHD. My next adventure is learning to take this cute little pill that Dr. Murphy has prescribed me................oh brother!

Jackson Approved: 50 Amazing Positive Affirmations

1. I am brave
2. I am smart
3. I am loved
4. I can do all things
5. I am capable
6. I am enough
7. I am uniquely me
8. I am wonderfully and fearlessly made
9. I am not afraid
10. I am handsome
11. I am beautiful inside and outside
12. I believe in myself
13. I love others
14. I will do my best; I am the best
15. I can be anything that I want to be
16. I am a hard worker
17. I will never give up
18. I am proud of myself
19. I am encouraged
20. I am fearless
21. I am strong
22. My life is important
23. I matter
24. I am special and important to so many people

25. I am prepared to succeed
26. I am amazing
27. I am grateful
28. I am happy
29. I am worthy and deserving of great things
30. I have what it takes to be successful
31. I determine the direction of my life
32. I am capable of making good choices
33. I am calm and patient
34. I am kind
35. I am positive
36. I am purposed
37. I am favored
38. I am destined for greatness
39. I am able to accomplish great things
40. I can do it
41. I will do it
42. I got this
43. I can handle this
44. I love myself
45. I am honest
46. I am special
47. I help others
48. I spread kindness everywhere I go
49. I am an important part of this world
50. I have special gifts to share with the world

Other Things Found in Jackson's Toolbox: 50 Healthy Coping Skills

1. Practice deep breathing- in through your nose, out through your mouth
2. Do a puzzle
3. Draw, paint or color
4. Listen to uplifting or inspirational music
5. Blow bubbles
6. Squeeze an ice cube tightly
7. Go to the library
8. Visit the animal shelter
9. Pet your cat or dog
10. Clean or organize a space
11. Make your bed
12. Play a game on the computer
13. Sit in the sun and close your eyes
14. Suck on a peppermint
15. Chew gum
16. Compliment someone
17. Read
18. Relax and think about happy, calming thoughts
19. Jump up and down
20. Write yourself a nice note and carry it in your pocket
21. Do the dishes
22. Go for a 10-minute walk
23. Dance to music
24. Call a family member or a friend
25. Organize your room or your books
26. Write positive affirmations on note cards & decorate

27. Go outside and listen to nature
28. Work in the garden or flower bed
29. Plant a flower in a pot
30. Watch a funny movie or funny show
31. Make a collage with pictures of your favorite things
32. Make a collage showing a positive future
33. Journal
34. Write a poem
35. Make a gratitude list
36. Scream into a pillow
37. Swim, run, jog, ride your bike
38. Jump rope
39. Play a musical instrument
40. Do a good deed
41. Shoot basketball
42. Sing your favorite song out loud
43. Count backwards from 100
44. Think of 3 foods for every letter or the alphabet without skipping any
45. Write down how you're feeling & why, read 1x & put it away
46. Visualization- close your eyes and imagine yourself in a beautiful place- how does it smell, what do you see, what do you hear, what do you feel...
47. Write something positive about yourself for every letter of the alphabet- decorate it & hang it where you will see it every day
48. Write a thoughtful and kind letter to someone
49. Pray or recite your favorite prayer
50. Read

Meet the Authors and Co-Authors

Shannell is a Licensed Professional Counselor and has worked in the mental health field since 2011. She has worked for the Georgia Crisis and Access line as a crisis counselor, she worked several years at an acute psychiatric facility, and she worked for a major health insurance company. She currently works in a private practice providing individual, couples, and family counseling services. Throughout the course of her work in mental health, she has worked with children, adolescents, adults, and seniors. She is a wife and the mother of Princeton.

Keva is an entrepreneur and a master cosmetologist who has been in the hair industry for over 19 years. During those years she became an educator in cosmetology. Additionally, she is a master barber and a Trichologist. She is the proud mother of two children, Kasey and Karter.

Latrice has experience in education that derives from over twelve years as an educator, with eight of those years being a classroom teacher of grades ranging from kindergarten to fifth grade. She holds an Educational Specialist Degree in Curriculum and Instruction, a Masters in Elementary Education (Grades 1-6), and a Bachelor of Science Degree in Mathematics. She is a highly-qualified educator certified in Early Childhood (K-5) and Middle Grades Math and Science. In addition to being a "school – mother", she is the mother of Chelcey.

Our Co-Authors

Kasey is an upcoming 11th grader. She loves cheering and hanging out with her friends

Chelcey is an upcoming 6th grader. She is a well-balanced honor roll student who loves playing basketball, softball, and Fortnite. She thrives off athletics, but more importantly spending time with her family and friends.

Karter is an upcoming 5th grader. He loves swimming, playing basketball, and playing Fortnite.

Princeton is an upcoming 2nd grader. He loves swimming, playing baseball, playing the piano, and playing Fortnite and Roblox. He loves math and he also enjoys reading books. Princeton is a principal's list recipient for making all A's this past school year. In 2018, he set a goal and read 100 books!

Made in the USA
Columbia, SC
17 July 2019